From the wild

MARY ANN ARCHIBALD

⁐

www.MaryAnn.ca

❧ FROM THE WILD ❧

CONTENTS

DEDICATION

This book is dedicated to you, dear reader, and to people who compress inspiration and observations into the written word. Then season these delicate vignettes in boxes and drawers for a time before returning them to the wild.

M.A.

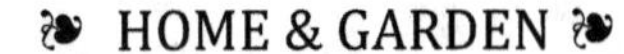 HOME & GARDEN

Fudge

I see my mother in a pot of fudge,
a hot, heavy pan and rhythmic wooden spoon.

Smiling and winking in the thickening sweetness
that sucks the air as the spoon comes up for breath
then back again into the heat for another beating.

The hot, round music of anticipation when you dig
your bottom teeth into the hardening sugar
and lick the spoon with your prickly burnt tongue.

It lasts two lifetimes
one for you
the other for when she is gone.

Summer notions

The hollow echo of a cottage
inner tubes, rubber ducks and clouds
turned out, lose on the ocean

Red, wet, sandy feet on waxy linoleum
leaves turned upside down on their branches
a thousand silver fishes scattering their airborne school

Everything shimmers against the dark grey-blue sky
that plays host to a puffy orange kite tugging at the wind
as it races you towards the grass.

Little green alien

For hours
the little white dog
with oil drop eyes
races back and forth
shakes the ball
that spills out of her mouth

With laser vision
she chases the ball
again
and again
through the fresh cut clippings
on a small patch of mown lawn
a little green alien.

Civic duty

I tuck him under my arm like a football
to avoid the salt that pierces and cripples his feet.

Occasionally, he gets a touchdown,
waters a snowbank that's still melting.

He runs like the wind
to the end of his leash
chasing hungry ducks
the city says we may no longer feed.

He tackles anything – a parked car with lights clicking, flashing,
a garbage bag liberated by the wind,
even you.

And beware he might lick you to death
or stare down a drooling Rottweiler
who could slurp him up like a five-pound bag of sugar.

People bark at him
usually burly joggers who pirouette and tippy-toe by
when he barks back at their ankles.

He does his business and I do mine: civic duty
pick up left-overs, toss them in a can,
wrap him up in my coat and carry him home again
like a football.

Here she is

She wears her glasses
on her head
like a tiara

Yellow rubber gloves
cover her elbows
and complete the ensemble

Victoriously she hoists her
brush, a sceptre of
divine cleanliness

Onward, charges
a sunbeam brandishing
oddities of dust particles
floating aimlessly.

Lemonade

Today was like
a lemon
I squeezed out its juice
added sugar, water, ice
and slipped in a straw.

Sweet rocket

Leaning in to tug a weed
I smell it

That thing ...
they try to bottle it

In your fabric softener,
for your dryer

A light, humid softness
as the dew rises

Sunshine rinses off
her curly purple hair

The earth heaves her
filtered bosom

A moist waft of breath
sixty-million-years-old

Brushes past your cheek
and the sweet rocket caresses your nose

Air a soft fabric
upon your skin

In this dewy spring moment
to savour until the next wash.

Mock orange evening

On being a girl who
loves enveloping my head
in the scent of the mock orange.

To close my eyes
and think about world peace
until I am dizzy.

From its fragrance
and greenery of possibility
with those vibrant white petals.

That light up the night
eclipsing fireflies
on a hot July evening.

❧

Forsythia's song

It's spring! It's spring!
The forsythia bring.

While the blue jays hark
and red breasted robin sing!

It's spring! It's spring!
Time to lay upon this earthy crust.

A seed, to sow
And grow a finer thing!

The yellow spires against a sky of blue and gold
The branches hold their trumpets high.

It's spring! It's spring!
The forsythia sing.

Scattered seeds

Scattered seeds the wind blows
a dandelion, phlox and marrow

Till to the bone, a harrowed row
yet the mortal coil, many seeds to sow.

❧ **NEAR & FAR** ❧

The traveller

The traveller greases the hinges
on his battered suitcase
yellowed, fat fingers melting in the heat
the plane, the air, the trays, the peanuts, the teeth.

Swipes away the rolling drips
his forehead, dark blue armpits
next to him, someone reading, and listening
earbuds and an intense gaze
that warns, without words, without rhyme,
"I am here for the duration"
"Do Not Disturb."

The flight will be a long one then
no chat, no buddy for a beer, a ball game, a joke
except a bumped elbow or arm
and a quick, stolen look and furrowed brow
back into the book.

From the battered suitcase
the traveller unleashes
an electronic zoo of cords
to prevent time from hovering
in the air 35,000 feet above the ground
and to continue the speed of sound with
"Ladies and gentlemen, this is your Captain"
plastic knife, spoon, fork
rubber lunch and three
dark rum and cokes 'til landing.

Dreamy duet

I couldn't sleep so we drove
the rough gravel
spewed dust in our path
taste of grit inside my cheek

I leaned into my Dad's arm
on the steering wheel
as he sang his rendition of
"Everybody loves somebody"

I closed my eyes and he
became Dean Martin
kept them closed and Ella
Fitzgerald joined in
"Everybody falls in love
somehow"

And we drifted into the night,
car tires fighting
rogue stones biting the metal
to try to thwart our armoured
vehicle.

the tin can
filled with love,
filled with song,
filled with sleep.

The slumber came to me
like pieces of confetti,
or falling stars,
or asteroids broken into
a thousand pieces on that
road.

Silent tires screech our arrival
home
the band was still.

Dean carried me into the
house.
I clung onto his neck,
awake but keeping my eyes
pinched shut.

Holding onto their dreamy
duet
until I was plunked into bed
my eyes open wide.

Can we go for another drive?
another overdue dream
from the sleep library.

❧

November

The month of November rings out
like a warning shot from a long rifle.
Shortened northern daylight
gathers the cool
reminders that winter,
its dark freeze, is on its way.

Better get ready
stockpile
prepare.

Autumn is almost over
carolling almost begun

Time to unwrap your long red and white striped
scarves and matching white maple-leaf mittens
cheer the game of shinny up at the rink
with chairs scratching the surface
toddlers earn their Canadian keep.

Knee high snow drifts under
yellow street lights hug the rink.

November, its that long shot month
the warning, winter's almost begun
the days are yet to get even shorter
Christmas lights rise on the horizon

Leaves fall to the ground
the warning shot is fired
winter's first blast has won another round. ❧

Snowflakes

Just when I think I'm alone.
Big, milky snowflakes foam.
Slushy froth covers the sidewalk.
Creamy white jazz hands.
Break my fall.
Under a buttery moon smiling down on me,
laughing.

Rejection collection: *The New Yorker* poem

So, I wrote to the New Yorker
And the New Yorker wrote back
We live, we breathe poetry
And you're not from our hood, Jack.

Do you even read our rag,
our riches, our rhyme?
If you had, if you'd taken
or spent more of your time.

You'd note, that we're famous,
we're polished, we're true
And if you ain't a New Yorker,
we ain't publishing you.

So here's your rejection
your diligence is due
enjoy your collection
in the future, get a clue.

34

Fireflies

There was a firefly
Or a hundred or so
In the clean night
That I caught in a jar

Rescued from the wilderness
blinking syncopation
buzzing and flickering
until I brought it

Into the yellow kitchen
and saw the magic evaporate
the light and the wall became one
and they were tiny. Bugs

With drooping wings
looking at me
through the jar

Bewildered by the light
that drowned their
blazing dance
leaving only a charred ember

no smoke or flame
until they were released
back into the indigo air
to fire up the night again.

Daybreak

Bumping the moon
onto our garden path
snuffing out fireflies

The dusty moon asleep,
a sliver in the sky
tucks away its cratered mirror

as the sun lights
the other side
and dark finds its dawn.

Sunset into night

Deep, low and golden
the sunset torches the sky
the sun and moon amplify its light
a dying dragon breath

grey clouds eclipse shining reflections
of sprinkled fireflies
floating over tender orbits
skippers dance on the surface
click and tip their glasses to
smiling stars, freckles rising,
twinkling in the night.

❧

Crashing the doe

before you were unbroken
from the impact and
things you've seen

on the drive home
after swimming in the desert

you had to scrub the sadness from your eyes
remove the broken glass,
shards of metal and steel bolts
that skewered your eyes
like broken headlights from crashing the doe.

The river

How the river would flow
the bear, the deer

Fresh green leaves
and lemon-lime grass
air fresh and soft

A nose twitch
no car, no noise
just gurgles

the river that flows
back from where it came
the glacier, the volcano.

❧

Rocky shoreline

The waves rush in
and the water's cold
silver pools
turn to islands of green and gold.

Saw dust days

Tall and angled,
a stream of shredded wood and
sun shine confetti, cascades
into a huge yellow swell
under a sun high in the blue

Climbing a mountain of golden wooden curls
in sneakers or gum rubber boots
flinging tiny parts of cabers overhead
as they patter back down
outstretched arms catch
warm flakes of moist pulp

The scent of fresh wood, shavings
cling to tanned skin
and tuck into sneakers, shirt, pants
slide back down, knee deep
celebrating the pony's fresh mattress

Spitting out flecks of yellow pulp
inhaled on the way up,
a bokah lens on your eyelashes
as you squint overhead into the sun
and the saw dust days of summer.

છ

Brave and stupid

Am going where only
bravery will take me and
stupid, my sidekick

We get along well.
Without them,
life would be boring.

Junior high

Burnt sewing machine oil fills the air
as coils of swirly blue fabric fall over the lip of the table
and inch-long threads fray the edges of the large diamond
of polyester, which would later become a sleeve
in those last bustling moments of home economics class.

You wrapped your arm around my shoulder
as I brushed your peach fuzz face
under the bubbled arch shrouded
in the bouquet of Aqua Velva
that scorched your tender face.

Vocal chords

The pain in his voice and rubbery face
the density of bone and human word
when he flew over the pot hole
on his childhood bike

His crotch hit the cross bar
and the handles punched his gut
knocked the wind
and pride right out of him

So fast
it came out in his voice
compressed, constricted
they knew and gave it away

"Are you okay?"

"Yep. Fine"

Spurts of sound tickled him
with a concrete feather and road rash
he couldn't admit it
so he kept it to himself
but not his vocal chords.

Old images

Look into the eyes of the past
grim faces stare back
they did not know
they were supposed to smile,
be skinny, seduce the camera,
pout a little.

Time

Time is a slippery predator.

Provides little warning
doesn't leave a scent.

Passing through us,
let's us know it was here.

Its trackless hooves shape-shift
our bodies,
our lives,
our being.

Hundred-year-old photos of lives
someday as real as our own
as real as time.

Through the past

The otherworldliness of days gone by,
sipping a cloud in a cup
to discover it is only air
drinking in the ether

Sounds of days gone by
voices calling in tongues long silenced
with deadened dialects

is a loin cloth a fad? A trend? A necessity?
Victorian lovelies wearing a flower for a hat.
heads covered in big black tulips
in those black and white
monochrome, faded photographs

Run your finger over the image
grasp its realness
only yesterday, a yesterday
their yesteryear that evaporated into that cup of clouded ether.

Gravity

You've been told but you didn't believe
until that day your eyelids fell heavy

and you wondered
"what is that?"

the droop persists the afternoon nap
gravity disease and belly folds

breasts lower
eyes downcast

a knee twists all that you took for granted
takes you down gravity wins

confirms

folds of skin in their heavy greyness
wrinkle and pull back the years

when you look in the mirror
and wonder who is looking back

through the triple pane
that holds your past, present, future

like when you run your fingers
through your head
of wired silk.

FROM THE WILD

Brass

polished notes
through corridors of brass
wind their way
through fields of melodies
raking corn
spearing fish
with nipped ears
hear bright yellow sound
flowing freely
bubbling along the
river's edge
of an elevator's interior

penthouse notes
of executive brass
work their way through fields of commodities
raking it in
spearheading deals
dripped tears
flow blood red
bubbling along a
child's face
on the edge
of the third interior

Dreamed I was dead

Dying
melting
like a sponge
a lost form
frayed edges.
a lost grip
no longer holding air
wrung out,
worry free.

On god and destiny

One god
which god
no god?
looking forward
looking back

Over your shoulder
to the other side
a test

Create your own
from dirt

One god?
No god?
The other?

Becoming

It is not my job
to make the butterfly
leave its cocoon

It is not my job
to calve the cows
at midnight

It is my job
to love
and be there

A witness to your world
my world
unfolds into our world.

Meditation

Breath,
a pebble
rising,
falling,
on my belly

Transform,
focus
calm,
serene,
in my mind

From the wild

mental meditation
images, ideas, concepts
montage, mosaic, collage, scent

shut out the noise
indulge
sound, voice, rhythm
song

turn down the hunger
feed it
a nourishing quest
soul, sanity, stomach
meal, medicine

stomp through words
peek under the hood
distant time
now, past, never

float
by unnoticed today,
on this rush, journey, path
pilgrimage

rest for your soul
for just one beat.

ACKNOWLEGDMENTS

This collection was previously published as *Poems: 20-cents each*. From the Wild represents the revised and complete version of that book.

Several of the poems in this collection were previously published. *Brass* was originally published in *The Amethyst Review*, a literary journal from Maliseet Press (1995: Truro, Nova Scotia). *Mock Orange Evening* was published in *Open Heart Forgery* (2010: Halifax, Nova Scotia) and is included in *Open Heart Forgery: Year One Anthology*.(ISBN 978-0-986861-0-6) and *Fudge* was published in *Open Heart Forgery* (2011: Halifax, Nova Scotia).

ABOUT THE AUTHOR

Mary Ann Archibald is published in radio, television, newspapers, magazines and online publications including: *The Chronicle-Herald, Outdoors Canada Magazine, Field & Stream, Truro Magazine, CBC Radio, WTN, Central Nova Business News, The Tatamagouche Light, Farm Focus of Atlantic Canada* and more.

Mary Ann's portraits, still life and landscape paintings are valued for their expressive, painterly and often lyrical qualities. She especially enjoys painting people and things from life and plein air landscapes. Her work is held in private collections throughout North America and Europe and in public collections with the province of Nova Scotia, Canada.

CONNECT

Enjoy this book? Please rate it and share your thoughts with one of the many online book review sites such as GoodReads.com or your online bookstore.

Want to be first to know about new releases by Mary Ann Archibald? Sign up for updates at www.MaryAnn.ca.

Twitter: @MaryAnnArch

Facebook.com/MaryAnnArch

www.MaryAnn.ca

www.ingramcontent.com/pod-product-compliance
Lightning Source LLC
Chambersburg PA
CBHW070451170726
48291CB00005B/1708